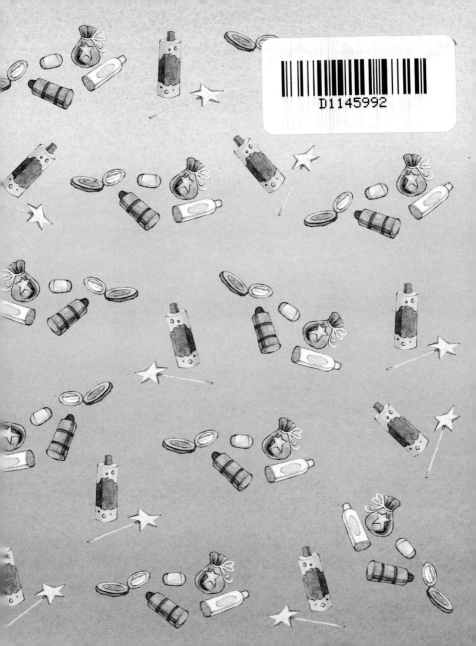

For Aunty Jo's nephews and nieces,
John, Alistair, Anya and Joseph.
Love Emma

Emma Thomson's
felicity Wishes®

FELICITY WISHES: BEAUTY MAGIC
by Emma Thomson

British Library Cataloguing in Publication Data
A catalogue record of this book is available from the British Library.
ISBN 0-340-88182-8
Felicity Wishes © 2000 Emma Thomson.
Licensed by White Lion Publishing.
Felicity Wishes: Beauty Magic © 2004 Emma Thomson.

The right of Emma Thomson to be identified as the author
and illustrator of this Work has been asserted by WLP
in accordance with the Copyright, Designs and Patents Act 1988.

First HB edition published 2004
10 9 8 7 6 5 4 3 2 1

Published by Hodder Children's Books, a division of Hodder Headline Limited,
338 Euston Road, London, NW1 3BH

Originated by Dot Gradations Ltd, UK

Printed in China
All rights reserved

Emma Thomson's
felicity Wishes®

Beauty Magic

*Hodder
Children's
Books*

A division of Hodder Headline Limited

Felicity landed on Holly's doorstep with an unfairy-like thud. She was carrying bags and bags of beauty products for the fairies' spa day at home.

Felicity's three giggling friends, Holly, Polly and Daisy, opened the door in a whirl of excitement.

"This is going to be so much fun," squealed Daisy.

"Are you sure you haven't forgotten anything?" said Holly jokingly, as they helped Felicity carry her heavy bags up the stairs to Holly's bedroom.

Felicity tipped the contents of her bags onto the bed.

"Wow! Where do we start?" said Polly, overwhelmed by all the colourful bottles.

Laden with lotions and potions, the fairy girls squeezed into Holly's bathroom, which really wasn't big enough for four sets of wings!

"The first treatment of our spa day," announced Holly, "is hair!"

Felicity, Polly and Daisy clapped their hands in excitement.

"Fairy Girl has a wonderful piece on how to wash your hair with a magical touch," said Holly, finding the right page.

"Let's take turns to wash each other's hair!" suggested Felicity, jumping up and down.

MAGIC RECIPE FOR SOFT AND SILKY HAIR

STEP 1 ~ Wash your hair with shampoo.

STEP 2 ~ Apply conditioner to the roots of your hair and then comb it through gently.

STEP 3 ~ Leave it in for a minute or two before rinsing with warm water.

STEP 4 ~ Pat your hair dry with a towel.

The fairy friends headed back to Holly's bedroom for the next part of their spa day.

"Let's do something whilst we wait for our hair to dry," said Polly.

"I have a great recipe for a face mask somewhere," said Felicity, rummaging in her bag. "Off to the kitchen!" she said, waving the recipe above her head.

A few minutes later, the fairies emerged in Felicity's homemade banana and honey face mask.

"This is yummy," whispered Daisy to Holly, as she licked a slice of banana off her face.

Felicity's Face Mask Recipes

CARROT AND HONEY (normal to oily skin)

Cook 3 large carrots, then mash them together.
Mix with 5 tablespoons of honey. Gently apply to face
and neck. Wash off with cool water after 8-10 minutes.

STRAWBERRY AND HONEY (oily skin)

Mash 8-10 strawberries with a fork. Mix with a tablespoon
of honey. Gently apply to face and neck. Rinse off with
cool water after 5 minutes.

BANANA AND HONEY (dry skin)

Mash 2 bananas and a tablespoon of honey together.
Gently apply to face and neck. Rinse off
with cool water after 10 minutes.

"What next?" asked Felicity,
from underneath her cucumber eyes.
"Massage!" said Polly, consulting Fairy Girl.
"Ooh! That sounds like a fabulous idea," said
Felicity. "I'm aching all over from carrying those
heavy bags."

So the fairy friends perched where they could
and eagerly waited for Polly to finish reading the
tips on massage techniques.

POLLY'S TOP MASSAGE TIPS

🌼 Make sure your friend is comfortable lying face down.

🌼 Use a soft, firm surface. A settee is too soft.

🌼 Use light to moderate pressure and a slow steady pace.

🌼 Use massage oil or body lotion to rub into the skin.

"Who wants to go first?" asked Polly finally.
"Me!" called out Felicity, Holly and Daisy
together as they all flung themselves onto Holly's bed.

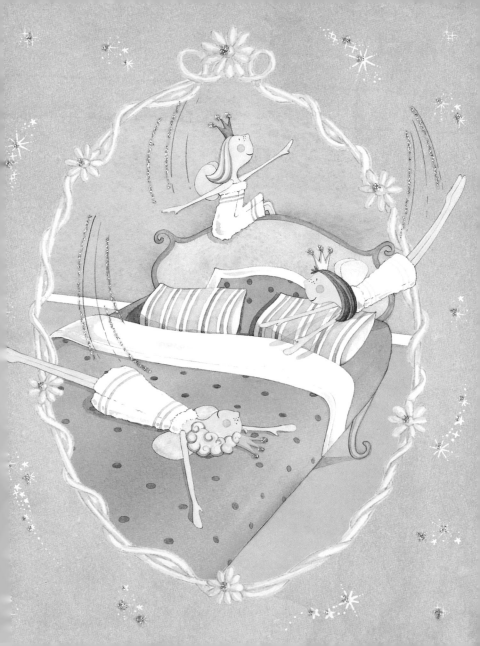

"What now?" asked Felicity, feeling relaxed.

"Feet!" said Daisy, picking up a bottle of fairy foot lotion. "It says here that happy feet make for a happy fairy!"

Felicity and her friends sat on the edge of the bath and soaked their feet in hot water. Then Daisy rubbed foot cream into Felicity's toes and ankles.

"Wow! I really do have twinkle toes!" exclaimed Felicity, admiring her smooth feet.

Polly tried to do the same to Holly's feet but every time she touched them, Holly wriggled away in fits of laughter.

DAISY'S TIPS FOR TWINKLE TOES

❀ Wash your feet daily with soap and water.

❀ Use moisturising cream on dry parts of your feet.

❀ Treat your feet to a foot massage every so often.

❀ Remember, happy feet make a happy fairy.

Felicity, Holly and Polly lay sleepily on Holly's bed.

"We haven't finished yet!" said Daisy. "The most important bit is still to come."

The fairy girls looked curiously at Daisy.

"Perfume, of course!" said Daisy, handing Holly a bottle.

"It doesn't smell very special," said Holly disapprovingly.

"That's because we haven't added the magical ingredient!" said Daisy, picking the petals off a delicate pink rose. "Fairy rose perfume!" she said, spraying the other fairies with the most beautiful scent.

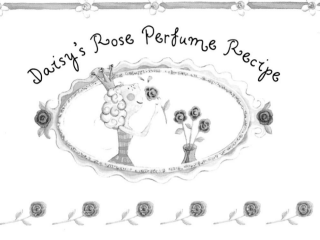

Daisy's Rose Perfume Recipe

YOU WILL NEED:
water, rose petals, kitchen tissue, a glass jar, a bowl, a sieve.

Collect rose petals and rinse them in cold water.

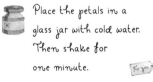

Place the petals in a glass jar with cold water. Then shake for one minute.

Place the jar on a window ledge in direct sunlight. Shake for one minute every day.

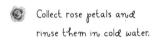

After a week, use a sieve to strain the perfume into a bowl. Then refill the jar with your perfume.

Before using the perfume test it on a small patch of skin to make sure you are not allergic to it.

"I never knew being beautiful could be so exhausting!" said Felicity, with a large sigh.

"I'm going to let you into a secret," said Holly. "We all know that fairies live forever but unless we take good care of our skin, we certainly won't look young forever."

Felicity, Daisy and Polly all looked at their faces in the mirror.

"But we're not old yet!" said Polly, slightly offended.

"Fairies are never too young to begin a daily routine," said Holly, passing around a tiny pink jar of moisturiser.

Glowing with beauty, the fairies carefully packed their slippers and towels. They didn't want their spa day to end.

"I feel so twinkly," said Daisy.

"Like a new fairy," said Polly.

"I wish we could have a spa day every day," said Felicity.

Suddenly, there was a large flash and the room filled with a sparkly light.

"Felicity, you made a wish!" gasped Holly. "You know as fairies we should only make wishes for the good of others and not for ourselves."

"But it's not for me!" said Felicity, holding up a paper scroll that had landed from nowhere on her lap. "It's a list of all the wonderful things we used for our spa day. Now every fairy can have a twinkly spa day just like ours."

Top Beauty Tips

1. Add a few drops of fairy perfume to your bath for a relaxing treat.

2. Always make sure you get a good night's sleep.

3. There is no need to buy expensive face masks. Make your own.

4. Apply a moisturiser to your face and neck every day.

5. Leave your hair to dry naturally whenever possible.

With this
beauty book comes an
extra special Felicity wish:

Open the book with your eyes
closed and let it fall open on any page.
Think of a wish you'd always dreamed
would come true and whisper it into
the page three times.

Keep this book in a safe place and,
maybe, one day, your wish
might just come true.

Love felicity
x